The New Adventures of
MARY-KATE & ASHLEY ™

The Case Of The
Golden Slipper

Look for more great books in

series:

The Case Of The Great Elephant Escape
The Case Of The Summer Camp Caper
The Case Of The Surfing Secret
The Case Of The Green Ghost
The Case Of The Big Scare Mountain Mystery
The Case Of The Slam Dunk Mystery
The Case Of The Rock Star's Secret
The Case Of The Cheerleading Camp Mystery
The Case Of The Flying Phantom
The Case Of The Creepy Castle
The Case Of The Golden Slipper

and coming soon
The Case Of The Flapper 'Napper

ATTENTION: ORGANIZATIONS AND CORPORATIONS
Most HarperEntertainment books are available at special quantity discounts for bulk purchases for sales promotions, premiums, or fund-raising. For information, please call or write:
Special Markets Department, HarperCollins Publishers, 10 East 53rd Street, New York, NY 10022
Telephone: (212) 207-7528. Fax: (212) 207-7222.

The Case Of The

Golden Slipper

by Melinda Metz

HarperEntertainment
An Imprint of HarperCollins*Publishers*

A PARACHUTE PRESS BOOK

PARACHUTE PRESS

Parachute Publishing, L.L.C.
156 Fifth Avenue
New York, NY 10010

DUALSTAR PUBLICATIONS

Dualstar Publications
c/o Thorne and Company
A Professional Law Corporation
1801 Century Park East
Los Angeles, CA 90067

▬HarperEntertainment

An Imprint of HarperCollins *Publishers*
10 East 53rd Street, New York, NY 10022

Copyright © 2000 Dualstar Entertainment Group, Inc. All rights reserved.
All photography copyright © 2000 Dualstar Entertainment Group, Inc.
All rights reserved.

THE NEW ADVENTURES OF MARY-KATE & ASHLEY, THE ADVENTURES OF MARY-KATE & ASHLEY, Mary-Kate + Ashley's Fun Club, Clue and all logos, character names and other distinctive likenesses thereof are the trademarks of Dualstar Entertainment Group, Inc. All rights reserved. THE NEW ADVENTURES OF MARY-KATE & ASHLEY books created and produced by Parachute Publishing, L.L.C., in cooperation with Dualstar Publications, a division of Dualstar Entertainment Group, Inc., published by HarperEntertainment, an imprint of HarperCollins *Publishers*.

If you purchased this book without a cover, you should be aware that this book is stolen property. It was reported as "unsold and destroyed" to the publisher, and neither the author nor the publisher has received payment for this "stripped book."

No part of this publication may be reproduced in whole or in part, or stored in a retrieval system, or transmitted in any form or by any means, electronic, mechanical, photocopying, recording, or otherwise, without written permission of the publisher.

For information, address HarperCollins Publishers Inc.,
10 East 53rd Street, New York, NY 10022.

ISBN 0-06-106593-5

HarperCollins®, ▬®, and HarperEntertainment™ are trademarks of
HarperCollins Publishers Inc.

First printing: November 2000

Printed in the United States of America

10 9 8 7 6 5 4 3 2 1

ROYAL INVITE

Very, very slowly, Ashley opened the thick, light pink envelope.

"Let me do it," I begged. The excitement was killing me. I reached for the envelope. It was addressed to the two of us.

"No way, Mary-Kate!" my twin sister answered. "You'll rip it. And I want the royal seal for our scrapbook."

I couldn't wait. I jumped up from my seat and raced around to the other side of the kitchen table. "Hurry, hurry, hurry!" I chanted. But Ashley didn't speed up at all!

Sometimes I can't believe how different Ashley and I are. We look exactly the same—same blond hair and blue eyes, same nose, same mouth. But in some ways we're total opposites. For example, I'm an envelope ripper. Ashley is a non-ripper. She puts her pinkie finger under the envelope flap. Then she carefully, *carefully* pulls the flap away from the rest of the envelope.

Finally, Ashley got the envelope open. She pulled out a darker pink card. It had gold trim all the way around it.

"What does it say?" I cried.

"You're not going to believe this!" Ashley answered. She read out loud: "'Princess Glorianna of Pomeroy requests the honor of your presence at her Friends of All Nations Ball on May twelfth at eight o'clock. The Marsdon Mansion, Old River, Georgia. Formal dress. RSVP.'"

"Princess Glorianna. Wow!" I breathed.

"I've seen her on TV. I can't believe she invited us to her ball!"

"I know!" Ashley cried. "A real princess! She's only thirteen, but she's so amazing. She travels all over the world and meets famous people."

"Mary-Kate! Ashley! I'm home," our mother called. A moment later she stepped into the kitchen. She held two boxes in her arms. "These are for you," she told us.

"What are they?" I asked.

"You'll have to open them and see," our mom answered. "I'm just the delivery person. They were on the front porch."

I grabbed the one with my name on it. I had it open in about two seconds. "Oh, wow!" I gasped. Inside was the most beautiful dress I'd ever seen. It was one of those long ones that go all the way to the floor. It was maroon satin and velvet, with tiny pearls around the neck and hem.

"My goodness, who would send you

something like that?" our mother asked.

"Princess Glorianna!" Ashley answered. She pulled out a matching dress in green.

"*The* Princess Glorianna?" our mother repeated. "Why would she send you dresses? We don't even know her."

"She invited us to a fancy ball," Ashley explained. "And she guessed our sizes perfectly," she added, holding up her dress.

"I bet she invited the whole family," I added. "You got an envelope with a royal seal, too." I picked up the envelope from the kitchen table and handed it to her.

Mom's a ripper, like me. She had the envelope open in a flash. "There are plane tickets to Georgia for the whole family in here," she told us. "It says that Princess Glorianna is giving a special ball for fifty outstanding kids from all over the United States. You two were chosen for your great detective work."

"All right!" I exclaimed. Ashley and I

slapped a high five. We run our own detective agency, Olsen and Olsen, out of our house. Our dog, Clue, helps us.

"You'll stay at the mansion for the whole weekend," our mom continued. "The rest of us will be staying at a hotel at the Red Balloons amusement park, nearby."

Ashley blinked and shook her head. "Am I dreaming?" she asked.

"We'll have to get you some gloves. And new shoes," our mom told us. "And you'll have to learn how to curtsy. It's not every day you get introduced to royalty."

Ashley and I grinned at each other. I could hardly believe this was happening. We, the Trenchcoat Twins, were going to meet a real, live princess!

Three weeks later, Ashley and I stood inside Marsdon Mansion. We were at the end of a long line of kids, all waiting to meet the princess.

"Can you see her yet?" Ashley asked.

"No," I replied. "There are too many kids in front of us."

"Isn't the mansion amazing?" Ashley looked around the huge drawing room.

"Look at that statue of Glorianna," I said.

"It's made of ice. Isn't that cool?" Ashley asked.

I giggled as the line moved forward. "Ice is always *cool*, Ashley," I told her. She cracked up.

A girl with dark brown hair turned around and smiled at us. "I'm so nervous about meeting the princess," she said.

A waiter glided up to us. He balanced a silver tray on one hand. "Would you ladies care for a cucumber sandwich?" he asked.

Each of us took one. The waiter glided away.

"I've never had a cucumber sandwich," the dark-haired girl confided.

"Neither have we," Ashley said. "But

they sure are awfully yummy!"

The line inched forward again. The girl moved up. Ashley and I followed her. I did a quick count. There were only twelve people ahead of us now. We were almost there!

The dark-haired girl turned back to us. "I'm Jen Diaz, by the way. Chess champ."

"I'm Ashley Olsen. And this is my sister, Mary-Kate. We're detectives," Ashley added.

We all took three steps forward. There were only six people ahead of us now. I was starting to feel a little nervous myself. I grabbed Ashley's hand and squeezed hard. We were about to meet the princess!

The waiter glided up again. "Would any of you care for a frosted chocolate cookie?"

I decided not to take a cookie. I didn't want to do my curtsy covered in chocolate crumbs!

Jen gulped. "I'm next. Wish me luck."

"You'll be great!" Ashley told her.

We watched as Jen stepped in front of the princess. People with cameras were blocking our way, so we still couldn't really see Princess Glorianna.

Jen gave a wobbly curtsy. A second later she hurried away.

"Mary-Kate and Ashley Olsen," a short man in a gray suit announced.

We moved to stand in front of Princess Glorianna. Ashley and I both curtsied. "It's a pleasure to meet you, your highness," Ashley said. Her voice trembled a little.

"Thank you so much for inviting us," I added. I looked up to smile at the princess.

She was so beautiful. Her curly black hair was pulled back from her face. And her green eyes matched the emeralds in her necklace perfectly.

The princess beckoned us closer. "I'm so glad you're here," she whispered. "I need to speak with you. I can't explain now. But I'm in danger. And I need your help."

TEA WITH A PRINCESS

"I bet the princess invited us to breakfast so she can talk to us alone," Ashley said. It was our first morning in the mansion. We hurried downstairs.

I couldn't believe I'd slept at all the night before. How could I, knowing we were having breakfast with Princess Glorianna? And that she needed our help?

We rushed down the carpeted hall that led to the breakfast room. At the door I knocked twice. A girl with black hair and bright green eyes answered. She looked a lot like the princess, except younger. I guessed she was about our age—ten.

"Hi. I'm Serena, Princess Glorianna's cousin," she said. "And that's Milo." She jerked her thumb at a skinny guy across the room. "He's making a special movie about Glorianna."

Milo didn't even look up when we walked in. He was busy setting up lights.

Serena led us across the room to a long table. It was covered with muffins and cakes and fruit. "Glorianna ordered every yummy thing we could think of," Serena told us. "She gets to do that because she's the princess. I think it's cool."

A door at the back of the room opened, and Princess Glorianna entered. Milo began filming. Ashley and I dropped into curtsies.

"Please, don't," the princess said. "Just think of this as breakfast with friends."

"We don't *have* breakfasts like this with

our friends," I blurted out. Then I blushed.

"That's why I invited you," Princess Glorianna answered. "I want to hear *everything* about what you do with your friends. Tell me what your school is like."

Ashley gave me a puzzled look as we sat down. The princess had told us she was in danger. We thought she invited us to breakfast to talk about her problem. But instead she wanted to talk about our school and our friends. What was going on?

"*I* want to hear everything about being a detective," Serena added. "Especially what kinds of clues you use to solve your cases. What's the best clue?"

"Well, um, fingerprints are an important kind of clue," Ashley said. "Because each person's fingerprints are different."

"Right. And, um…" I shot a quick glance at Milo. He had the camera pointed straight at me. "And, um—"

"Don't pay any attention to him," Glorianna

said. "I know it's hard. But you get used to it."

"Why is he filming us?" Ashley asked.

The princess smoothed back her long dark hair. "My mother wanted him to make a movie of my trip. I've been traveling from country to country on a goodwill tour. My parents usually make the trip themselves every few years. But they were needed at home this time."

"So Glorianna came instead," Serena added. "It's part of being a princess. I think it's so much fun!"

"You only think it's fun because you don't have to do it all the time," Glorianna answered. "No one knows who you are. You can go to the mall without everyone staring at you."

"She's right." Serena stuck one foot up in the air so we could see her orange sneaker. "I bought these at the mall yesterday."

"Don't you just love them?" Glorianna asked Ashley and me.

"I'd let you borrow them," Serena told her cousin. "But you wouldn't be able to wear them." She turned to Ashley and me. "I'm big for my age. Glorianna's feet and mine are actually the same size. But Glorianna only wears golden slippers," she explained.

Milo gave a loud sigh. "Boring. Boring, boring, boring," he said. Each "boring" was louder than the last.

He tugged on his pointy beard. "You are sitting around talking about *sneakers*. That does not make a good film."

Glorianna raised one eyebrow. "My parents asked you to make your movie. But that does not mean I will speak only about what interests *you*."

"You get to be bossy when you're a princess. And even more bossy when you're queen," Serena whispered. "It's so awesome."

"Fine!" Milo snapped. "But don't be surprised if I get fired. It won't be my fault if this film is dull, dull, dull!"

Milo stomped out of the room. Glorianna and Serena giggled. "I'm so glad he's gone," the princess said.

Ashley gave me a little kick under the table. I knew exactly what she was thinking. *Now* Glorianna would be able to tell us her secret.

Glorianna picked up the teapot and poured tea for each of us. I was a little scared to pick up my cup. The china was so thin I could almost see through it.

"I know Serena has more questions about being a detective," Glorianna said. "But there's something I need to ask first."

I gave Ashley a little kick. *Here comes the secret!* I thought.

"Have you two ever been to Red Balloons, the amusement park near the mansion?" Glorianna continued.

Ashley and I stared at each other. "Huh?" I asked.

"I just want to know what it's like," Glorianna said. "I've never been to an amusement park."

It must be some secret, I thought. *She doesn't even want to talk about it in front of her own cousin.*

"Is Pomeroy so different from America?" Ashley asked.

Glorianna shook her head. "Not really. It's just that I have so many duties. I never have any time to myself."

"Yeah," Serena jumped in. "Glorianna has to meet all kinds of famous people. And cut ribbons with big scissors at ceremonies."

Ashley took a sip of tea. "Don't you like any of those things?" she asked Princess Glorianna.

"Of course," Glorianna said quickly. "And I'm proud to represent my people. It's an honor."

The door to the parlor swung open. A

tall, gray-haired man stepped in.

Princess Glorianna stood up. "This is my great-uncle, the duke of Ellington. On this trip, he's also the head of security."

The duke nodded to me and Ashley. Then he turned to Princess Glorianna. "It's time for your press conference," he told her.

"Please excuse me," Princess Glorianna said. She walked around the table. As she passed me she dropped a note in my lap. Then she hurried from the room.

My heart beat faster. I unfolded the note. I kept it under the table so that only Ashley could see it.

Dear Mary-Kate and Ashley, it said. *Meet me in my room at midnight. We must talk—alone. It's a matter of life and death!*

3

A BURNING SECRET

The rest of the day flew by in a blur. We went on a boat ride on a lake and played croquet with the other kids. But I couldn't stop thinking about Princess Glorianna. What could her problem be? It definitely sounded serious!

At last it was eleven forty-five—almost time to meet the princess. Ashley and I were in our room. We were supposed to be asleep.

I sat up a little straighter in my canopy

bed. "I can't believe this mansion holds all fifty kids," I said.

All the girls were on our floor. The boys were on the floor below us. The princess and her people were above us. Milo, too.

"This place is huge," Ashley agreed. "There must be at least forty bedrooms."

"Plus the ballroom, and three drawing rooms, and the kitchen, and two parlors, and the dining room...." I gave a huge yawn. "All this counting is making me sleepy."

"You can't fall asleep now," Ashley reminded me. "Here—listen to this." She held up a book. "In Princess Glorianna's biography it says that she has one hundred pairs of golden slippers."

"Whoa. And only one pair of feet," I answered.

Ashley threw a pillow at me. I threw it back.

"When Glorianna was a little girl she got

a pair of golden slippers as a present," Ashley continued. "The people in her country loved the pictures of her in the slippers. So her parents decided she'd always wear golden slippers."

"At breakfast today it sounded like she wished she could wear something else," I said.

"Yeah," Ashley answered. Her eyes didn't leave the pages of the book. "Listen to this: 'Glorianna is next in line for the throne.' That means she'll be queen of Pomeroy someday."

"What if something happened to her?" I asked. The thought sent a little shiver through me.

Ashley ran her finger down the page. "Then Serena would get to be queen," she answered.

"I bet Serena would love that. Not that she'd want anything bad to happen to Princess Glorianna," I added quickly.

"Serena would just like all the fancy food and clothes."

"And meeting all the famous people. And cutting the ribbons at ceremonies. And all the other stuff," Ashley added.

"What else does the book say?" I asked.

Ashley flipped ahead a few more pages. "It says Princess Glorianna has done a lot of charity work. She sold some of her jewelry to pay for a pet hospital. She also took a course in fire safety, then went on TV and explained what to do if there was a fire. Plus she started an adopt-a-grand-parent program."

"That's really great," I said. "I wonder if—" The alarm clock on the table next to my bed went off. "It's five minutes to mid-night," I told Ashley. "Time to go."

We climbed out of our beds. Then we crept out of our bedroom on tiptoe.

"We go up those stairs," I told her. "Then down the hall. Then right. It's the second

door on the left, I think."

We started down the hall. The mansion was very, very quiet.

"Do you smell something funny?" Ashley asked.

I gave a sniff. "It smells kind of like a barbeque," I answered.

"No. It smells like smoke!" Ashley exclaimed. She started to run. I was right behind her.

We raced upstairs, down the hall and around the corner. Smoke was pouring out from under the second door on the left.

"That's Glorianna's room!" I cried. "It's on fire!"

4

KIDNAPPED!

"**F**ire!" Ashley shouted.

Footsteps pounded behind us. Milo shoved his way past. He had his camera pointed at Princess Glorianna's door.

Serena burst out of the room across from Glorianna's. "Where's my cousin?" she cried. "Is she in her room?"

"Call the fire department!" I yelled. "Where's the closest phone?"

Princess Glorianna's door flew open. "Everyone calm down," the princess ordered. She held up a fire extinguisher. "The fire is out."

Milo rushed up and knelt in front of her. His camera whirred. He kept filming while Serena wrapped her cousin in a tight hug.

"Oh, Glorianna," Serena sobbed. "I'm so glad you're not hurt."

"Shhh," Glorianna said. "I'm fine." She gave Milo an annoyed look, but he didn't put down the camera.

"How did the fire start, Princess Glorianna?" Ashley asked.

Glorianna's face was pale. "I don't know," she answered. Her voice was very shaky.

I looked at Ashley. Ashley looked at me. I knew we were thinking exactly the same thing. Was the fire connected to the danger that Princess Glorianna was in?

"We need to search that room for clues. The sooner the better," Ashley whispered.

I nodded. "We should do it right now."

We started to go into the princess's room. Then a voice stopped us in our tracks. "Everybody back to bed!"

I turned and saw the duke striding toward us. "Milo, turn that camera off, and go back to your room," he ordered. "Glorianna will move into the bedroom next to mine. I want her sleeping there the rest of our stay."

Milo lowered his camera. He didn't look happy about it.

"I'll see you later," Princess Glorianna said to me and Ashley. Then she and Serena went off down the hall.

Ashley and I started to go into the princess's room again.

"Where do you two think you're going?" the duke barked.

We turned to face him. "We thought it would be a good idea to investigate how the fire started," Ashley answered.

"Of course," the duke said. "But I'll take

care of that. *I'm* the head of security, after all."

"We'd really like to help," I told him.

He smiled and shook his head. "It's much too late for you girls to be up. Now run along. I can handle this on my own."

We didn't have any choice. We turned around and headed back to our room.

"It's a good thing Princess Glorianna knows so much about fire safety," Ashley said. "If she hadn't learned how to use a fire extinguisher..." She shook her head.

We reached our room and climbed back into our beds. "I'll set the alarm for eight, okay?" I asked. "We need to talk to the princess as soon as possible."

"Good idea," Ashley answered. "What happened tonight proved she really needs our help. She *is* in danger."

Bang! Bang! Bang!
My eyes flew open. I checked the clock.

It was almost eight A.M.

"Mary-Kate! Ashley! Wake up!" a high voice cried. Someone banged on our door three more times.

I rolled out of bed and rushed to the door. Ashley was half a step behind me. "Who's there?" I asked.

"It's Serena!"

I jerked the door open. Serena opened her mouth to speak, but no words came out. She just burst into tears.

"What's wrong?" Ashley asked. She gently pulled Serena into our room.

Serena wiped her face with the back of her hand. I stared. She was wearing mittens with her nightgown!

I thought it was weird—especially since it wasn't winter. But right now I was more concerned with why she was crying.

Ashley pulled over a chair. Serena sat down and took a deep breath. "I can't find Glorianna anywhere!" she burst out. "I think something bad has happened to her!"

"Where have you looked?" Ashley asked.

"Everywhere!" Serena wailed.

"Then we'll have to look everywhere again," I told her.

"Come on." Ashley led the way out of the room. We almost ran into Milo. He had his camera pointed at us.

"What's going on?" he asked.

"Glorianna's missing!" Serena cried. "And the room she slept in—it looks like there was a fight in there."

"Don't worry. We're going to find her," Ashley said firmly. "Let's go."

She wasn't talking to Milo, but he decided to follow us anyway. And he didn't stop filming.

"Let's start with the room the princess moved into last night," I said. "Maybe we can find some clues there."

Serena broke into a run. "I'll show you where it is," she called over her shoulder.

Ashley and I raced after her. Milo stuck to us like glue.

We flew down the hall. Then up the flight of polished wooden stairs. Then down another hall and around the corner. Serena skidded to a stop in front of a door that was painted gold.

"This is it," Serena said breathlessly.

We followed her inside. My heart started beating double-time as I looked around the room. A chair lay on its side. The bedspread was torn off the bed. A lamp with a china base lay on the floor, broken into a hundred pieces.

"Serena, Milo, it might be better if you waited outside," Ashley said. "I'm sure there are a lot of clues here. Too many people in the room will make the clues harder to find."

"What's going on in here?" a loud voice demanded. The duke marched into the room. He stopped short when he saw the

huge mess that had been made.

"What happened?" he cried.

He reached down to pick up the chair.

"Wait! Don't move that," I said. I hurried over to the chair. I started to lower it back to the spot where it had been lying. Then I spotted a folded piece of light pink paper under it.

I picked it up by the edges and opened it. Letters had been cut out of a magazine. Then they'd been glued to the sheet of paper to make sentences.

I gasped as I read the message. "Ashley, you have to see this!"

She rushed over. I held the note in front of her.

"Oh, no!" she exclaimed. "The princess has been kidnapped!"

5

A FALSE CLUE

"**G**ive me that!" the duke snapped. He ripped the piece of paper out of Ashley's hands.

His eyes widened as he read the note. "It says that tomorrow I'll get a call," he said. "They'll tell me how much money it will take to get the princess back. We're not supposed to do anything until then. Especially not call the police."

"But you *are* going to call them, aren't you?" Ashley asked. "We shouldn't try to

handle this alone. A princess is missing!"

"The note says no police," the duke said. "Glorianna will be in danger if we call them."

"I agree," Milo added. He kept on filming.

"But the police will know how to catch the kidnappers," I said. "They're trained for stuff like that."

"No!" Serena wailed. "What if they make a mistake? We can't call them. We can't do anything that might hurt Glorianna!"

The duke put the note in his pocket. "Who is the head of security?" he asked us in a grumpy voice. Then he answered his own question. "I am the head of security. And *I* will handle the situation."

"Now this is interesting," Milo said. He filmed a close-up of the broken lamp. "Finally, something that isn't boring, boring, boring."

"Milo, turn off the camera," the duke ordered. He turned to Ashley and me. "And you two, go to breakfast. Then run along to the dog show with the other children."

Serena wiped her tears away with her mittens. I made a mental note to ask her about those mittens later.

"I guess I'll have to judge the show, since Glorianna's not here," Serena said. She sighed. "I'll need to wear one of her tiaras. And maybe even a pair of her golden—"

"That won't be necessary," the duke broke in. "I'll tell everyone that the princess has the flu."

Serena nodded and started for the door. Then she turned back to the duke. "What about the ball?" she exclaimed. "It's tomorrow night!"

"Glorianna will be home safe and sound by then. You can count on it," the duke said. He straightened his tie. "After all, I *am* the head of security."

"I really think if we call the police—" Ashley began.

"Thank you, girls," the duke said. "But I can take it from here. Run along. You don't want to miss breakfast. And remember—not a word about this to anyone!"

"You know what?" Ashley said once we were outside the princess's bedroom. "I'm not really hungry."

"Me either," I told her. "I can't wait to start working on the case. But how? We can't even get near the crime scene!"

"Did you notice that the window in the room was broken?" Ashley asked. "That must be how the kidnapper got in. Let's look for clues in the garden outside the princess's room."

"Good idea!" I said.

We hurried to our room and got dressed. A few minutes later, we were in the garden. We stared up at the windows on the fourth floor.

"That one is Princess Glorianna's," I said. I pointed to a broken window.

"Let's check the ground under it," Ashley said. "There may be footprints."

We pushed our way through the bushes along the side of the mansion lining the wall. Then we began to scan the ground. We didn't have to look very hard to find our first clue.

"Ashley!" I called. "Look!" I held up a golden slipper.

"That's Glorianna's shoe. Her right shoe," Ashley said. "They must have carried her out through the window." She frowned and scanned the ground some more. "I wonder how they got her down. I don't see any ladder marks."

Then she stopped and picked something up. "Here's a piece of glass from the window," she said.

"That's weird," I told her. "Why is the glass out here?"

"Huh?" Ashley's forehead wrinkled.

"If you break a window from the

outside, the glass falls *inside*, right?"

"Right!" Ashley exclaimed. "So the window must have been broken from *inside* the room. That's why the glass is out here!"

"But why would someone break the window to get *out*?" I asked. "It doesn't make sense. Unless…"

"Unless it was someone who was trying to make it *look* like they came from outside," Ashley finished for me. "Maybe it was someone who was already in the mansion. Someone who has no problem getting in. Because they're staying there."

I felt a chill go up my spine. "You mean…the kidnapper could be someone we know!"

6

CROWNING THE SUSPECTS

Ashley and I walked around to the front of the mansion. We sat on a bench under a big tree.

Ashley pulled out her detective notebook and a pencil. "I think you're right," she told me. "The kidnapper must be one of the people who's staying at the mansion. Let's make a list of suspects."

"I really like Serena," I began. "But..."

"But she's at the top of the list," Ashley finished. "She's always talking about how cool it would be to be the princess. And she *will* be the princess if anything happens to Glorianna." Ashley wrote down Serena's name.

"Let's ask the detectives for help," a voice called.

I jerked my head up. Jen Diaz was heading toward us. A tall blond girl named Caitlin was right behind her.

"Hey, you two," Jen said. "My favorite sweatshirt disappeared. It has bunnies playing chess on it."

"And my best pair of jeans is missing," Caitlin added. "They're bright orange."

"Weird!" I said.

"We need detectives to help us find them," Jen said. "We've looked everywhere!"

"When was the last time you saw them?" I asked.

"I don't know." Caitlin shrugged. "Last night, I guess. When I unpacked my jeans."

"That's when I last saw my sweatshirt, too," Jen said. "Oh, and one of the boys said his sunglasses have disappeared," she added.

Caitlin glanced at her watch. "We have to hurry or we'll miss the bus to the dog show. Are you guys coming?"

"We're, uh, we're going to stay here," I answered. I remembered that we weren't supposed to tell anyone about Glorianna disappearing. "But we'll look around for your stuff."

"We'll let you know if we find anything," Ashley promised.

"Thanks. See you later, then." Jen smiled and gave us a wave. She and Caitlin headed off.

"Okay, back to our suspects list," Ashley said.

"All that talk about clothes reminded me of something," I told her. "Don't you think it was a little strange that Serena was wear-

ing mittens inside the house?"

"Hey, yeah. Maybe she was wearing mittens because she didn't want to leave fingerprints!" Ashley said. "Remember how she was really interested when I told her that fingerprints are a very important clue?"

I frowned. "There's just one problem. Serena wouldn't need to keep her mittens on *after* the princess was kidnapped."

"True," Ashley agreed. She bit her pencil. "I still think the mittens are a good clue. But we have to think about all the possible suspects. How about Milo?"

I started drawing in the dirt with the toe of my sneaker. "Well, he's around the princess a lot. His room is even on the same floor as hers. But why would he kidnap her?" I wondered. "I mean, he needs her to be in his movie."

"But before the kidnapping his movie was boring, boring, boring," Ashley said. "This makes it a lot more interesting." She nodded. "He definitely belongs on the list." She wrote Milo's name in her notebook. "Any other suspects?"

"Well," I said. "Didn't you think it was weird that the duke didn't want to call the police?"

"Yes," Ashley agreed. "But why would he—"

"Uh-oh." I grabbed Ashley's arm. "Here he comes now! We can't let him see us. He'll make us go to the dog show."

We jumped off the bench. Then we scurried behind some bushes.

The duke walked past. He held a bunch of papers in one hand. He was reading the top one. He didn't notice us. He didn't even notice when he dropped one of his papers. But we did.

Ashley and I stayed still until he was out of sight. Then Ashley grabbed the paper he had dropped. We sat down on the bench again to look it over.

"It's a list of ways to make the mansion safer," Ashley explained. "Cameras. Guard dogs. Patrols." She flipped over the sheet of paper. "Hey! Look at this!" she exclaimed.

I leaned closer. It was a letter from the duke's bank.

"It says they're closing his royal bank account," Ashley told me. "He has no money left at all."

"He's definitely suspect number three!" I said. "The duke needs money. And the kidnapper is going to be asking for money tomorrow."

Ashley wrote the duke's name in her detective notebook. "I think he's an even better suspect than Serena."

"All three of our suspects have great motives," I answered.

"Motive" is a word detectives use a lot. It's a person's reason for committing a crime.

I stood up. "We have a lot to do. We need

to check out Serena, Milo, and the duke. And we have to get the princess back before the ball tomorrow night."

Ashley stood up. "There's something else we need to check out," she said. "I can't stop thinking about that fire last night. The fire and the kidnapping were only a few hours apart. Don't you think that's strange?"

I snapped my fingers. "Maybe the kidnappers set the fire!" I exclaimed. "Maybe they thought it would keep everyone busy. Then they could sneak Princess Glorianna out of the mansion."

"But it didn't work," Ashley added. "Because the princess put the fire out too quickly! So they had to come back later." She grabbed my arm. "Come on. Let's go check the first bedroom for clues."

She led the way back inside and up to the first room that Princess Glorianna had stayed in. The door was open a crack. I

reached for the doorknob. Ashley grabbed my wrist.

"Wait. There's somebody in there," she whispered.

We leaned forward and peered through the crack. I couldn't stop a little gasp from coming out of my mouth.

Serena sat on the floor, surrounded by beautiful gowns, golden slippers, and sparkling jewels. She picked up a tiara and set it on her head. "Welcome to my ball," she said to an imaginary crowd. "I hope you will all have a magnificent time."

Ashley and I slowly backed away from Glorianna's room. "Serena's already acting like she's the princess!" I whispered. "She's got to be the kidnapper!"

7

HIDING HER HIGHNESS

"**M**ary-Kate, slow down. I agree that Serena is an even better suspect now," Ashley whispered back. "But we don't have proof."

That's Ashley for you. She's so logical!

She sighed. "Let's go talk to her. Maybe she can explain."

I nodded. Then I rushed into the room. "What are you doing, Serena?" I cried.

Serena glanced up and waved. She didn't look guilty at all.

"Don't worry," she said. "I'm wearing mittens."

"Huh?" I said.

"Huh?" Ashley repeated.

"I'm checking Glorianna's clothes. I wanted to see if anything's missing," Serena explained. "But don't worry. I'm not getting fingerprints all over the place."

She waved her hands so we could see the mittens. "I put these on the second I knew Glorianna was missing. I remembered that you said fingerprints are an important clue. So I didn't want mine to get mixed up with the kidnapper's."

"Why are you wearing Glorianna's tiara?" Ashley asked.

"I was practicing for the ball," Serena admitted. She pulled the tiara off her head. "I was afraid Glorianna might not be back before tomorrow night. So I was practicing her welcome speech. I thought I might have to give it for her."

Ashley gave me a quick okay sign. She was telling me she believed Serena's story.

I nodded. I believed Serena, too.

"What have you found out?" I asked. "Is anything missing?"

Serena wrinkled her forehead. "Well, there are forty ball gowns. Twenty-seven tiaras. That's right. But there are only ninety-nine pairs of golden slippers—and this," she said, holding up a single golden shoe. "I don't know what happened to the other one."

I showed her the golden slipper we'd found in the garden. "We think this must have fallen off Glorianna's foot as the kidnappers took her away," I said.

"Well, that makes one hundred pairs," Serena said. "None missing."

But Ashley was shaking her head, looking puzzled. "That's weird," she said. "Why is the left shoe here? Shouldn't it be wherever Glorianna is?"

"That is weird," I agreed. The left slipper wasn't even in the room Glorianna had disappeared from. That meant she hadn't been wearing it when she disappeared. But she'd been wearing the other slipper, the right one.

Why had she worn only one shoe?

"The only other thing missing is something of mine," Serena said. "My new sneakers."

I frowned. "Lots of other kids are missing clothes, too," I told Serena. "There's a clothesnapper around here."

"Time to look for clues," Ashley said. "You take that half of the room, Mary-Kate. I'll take this half."

I carefully studied every inch of my half of the room. I was looking for anything out of place. A scrap of paper. A piece of cloth. Anything.

"There's the right number of pajamas, too," Serena called out from the closet.

"And the right number of day dresses. I don't think any of Glorianna's clothes are missing."

"Thanks, Serena," Ashley said. "We'll take it from here."

"Okay, see you later." Serena waved as she left the room.

I continued my search. One section of the wallpaper had dark streaks on it. I figured that was from the smoke last night. But everything else looked normal. No clues here.

I sighed. I couldn't help feeling disappointed.

Then Ashley rushed over to me. She looked very excited. She grabbed me by the elbow and pointed at the wallpaper. "Mary-Kate, look! Can't you see?" she cried.

8

A ROYAL PAIN

I stared at the wall. "What do you mean?" I asked Ashley.

"The wallpaper isn't burned," Ashley said. "Smoke messed it up, but it was never on fire."

"So?" I asked. "Nothing in here is burned."

"Exactly!" Ashley said. "Don't you think that's strange?"

"I guess so," I said. I was beginning to see her point. You can't have a fire without something burning.

"Something definitely should have been burned, Mary-Kate," Ashley said. She bit her lip. "Unless...maybe somebody cleaned up the room after the fire. Probably one of the maids took out everything that was burned."

"Great," I said. "That means we *still* don't have a clue."

"We searched all day, and we didn't find any clues. We still don't have any idea who kidnapped Glorianna—or where she is!" I complained. I stared up at the canopy of my bed.

"We can't give up," Ashley said. "There has to be something else we can check out."

Someone knocked on the door. A second later a girl with curly red hair poked her head into the room. "Hi. Jen said I should tell you guys that my lucky baseball cap is missing."

I opened my mouth to answer. But the girl disappeared before I could say anything.

Ashley was lying across her bed. Suddenly she sat up. "I know what to do!" she exclaimed. "Remember we talked about the maids cleaning up Glorianna's room? We have to go through the garbage! There are big Dumpsters by the back fence. I saw them yesterday."

She jumped up and raced over to the closet. A second later she was changing into an old pair of jeans. "Come on, Mary-Kate."

"Dumpsters are smelly," I reminded her.

"I know they're smelly," Ashley said. "But we could find a clue that will tell us who set the fire. And that clue could lead us straight to the kidnapper."

"Okay." I sighed. I grabbed my backpack. Then I reached for my sneakers. "Anything to find the princess."

It was after ten o'clock when we sneaked downstairs.

"There should be a back door leading from the kitchen," Ashley whispered. She hurried down the marble hall floor. Her sneakers squeaked with each step. So did mine. What if someone heard us?

We walked down a long hall to the kitchen. It smelled like freshly-baked cookies.

"Look how big that stove is," Ashley whispered. "It's like a stove for a restaurant. Not a house."

"I wish we had time for a cookie," I said. But we didn't. We hurried to the back door. Then we slipped outside.

The scent of flowers immediately filled my nose. The gardens at the mansion were huge! It was like being in a park.

"That's where we need to go," Ashley said. She pointed to a gravel path. High hedges ran along either side of it.

Crunch. Crunch. Crunch.

Our feet made a lot of noise on the gravel.

Crunch. Crunch. Crunch. "Grrr."

I froze. "Did you hear that?" I cried.

"What?" Ashley asked.

"Something growling," I answered.

"I didn't hear anything. Let's go," she said. "I can see the Dumpsters."

Crunch. Crunch. Crunch. "GRRRR."

Ashley stopped. "I heard *that*," she said.

"GRRRRR."

The sound was coming from behind us. Slowly I turned around. Two pairs of black eyes stared back at me.

"Oh, no!" I moaned. "Ashley, remember the duke's list? The list of ways to make the mansion more secure?"

"Yeah," Ashley said in a tense voice. "So?"

"So I think he already got the guard dogs!" I said.

9

ON THE SCENT...

"**A**shley, run!" I yelled. "We have to hide!"

"Get in one of the Dumpsters!" Ashley shouted. "The dogs won't be able to reach us in there."

I locked my eyes on the closest Dumpster as I ran.

"*GRRRRR. GRRRRR-R-R-R-UFFFF!*"

It sounded as if the dogs were right behind us!

"Just a little farther," Ashley gasped. "I'll

boost you up. Then you pull me in."

She reached the Dumpster an instant before I did. She crouched down and locked her fingers together. I jammed my foot onto her hands and jumped.

I grabbed the top of the Dumpster. Then I hauled myself into it. "Peeee-yew!" I groaned as the smell hit me.

"Hurry, Mary-Kate!" Ashley begged.

I leaned down and grabbed Ashley by the wrists. I yanked her up as hard as I could. The dogs were snapping at her feet!

Ashley tumbled into the Dumpster—and knocked me into something squishy.

"Yuck!" I said.

"We made it!" Ashley cried.

I could hear the dogs jumping up against the Dumpster. We finally got them to stop barking. Luckily, the side of the Dumpster was too high for them to jump over.

Ashley and I stood up inside. We pulled our flashlights out of our packs. We flicked them on and peered around at the garbage.

"Let's look for clues," I said. "Maybe the dogs will leave by the time we're done."

"They probably will," Ashley answered. But she didn't sound all that sure.

"I'll start looking at this end." I waded over to the right side of the Dumpster. "You start at the other one."

"Sounds good," Ashley answered.

"But it doesn't *smell* good," I complained. I took a pair of gloves out of my backpack and put them on.

"Remember, we're looking for anything that's been burned," Ashley said.

Most of the trash was in bags. I ripped open the closest one. Then I turned it upside down.

A shower of garbage fell out. It was so disgusting. I saw a fish head. Some half-eaten corn on the cob. A slimy head of lettuce. An empty milk carton. Gross. "This bag was all kitchen trash," I said. "Nothing here."

I ripped open another bag. This time, a bunch of crumpled-up paper fell out. None of it looked burned, though.

I opened a third bag. "This is the worst," I moaned as all kinds of slop came pouring out. But no clues.

It looked as if I'd just made a batch of stew in the Dumpster. Really bad stew. There were potato peelings. And brown gunk. And some steak bones. And some yellow gunk. And—

"I think I found something," Ashley exclaimed. "Come look!"

I waded through the sea of garbage to Ashley. She held up a small metal trash can.

I looked inside. All I could see was white powder.

"I think this white stuff is from the fire extinguisher," Ashley said.

I slid one hand through the powder. I felt something hard and round. I pulled it free and held it up so Ashley could see it.

"It looks like a smoke bomb," I said. "Remember the ones Samantha and Tim had at Halloween?"

"You're right!" Ashley exclaimed. "That's why nothing was burned in Princess Glorianna's room. There wasn't really a fire. There was only smoke!"

"Now we just have to figure out which of our suspects set off the smoke bomb," I said.

Ashley peered over the edge of the Dumpster. "The dogs are still down there," she said. "How are we going to get back to the mansion?"

"I know!" I exclaimed. "Bones!" I stumbled back across the Dumpster. I grabbed a steak bone in each hand. "What do you think?" I asked.

"I think you're brilliant, Mary-Kate!" Ashley answered.

"Hey, doggies! Look! Yummy bones for you!" I held up the bones. Both dogs

started to whine and slobber.

"Throw them over there, as far as you can," Ashley said. She pointed away from the house. "Then we'll run as fast as we can the other way."

"Okay. Here goes," I called. "One. Two. Three." I flung the bones. The dogs lunged for them. Ashley and I scrambled out of the Dumpster and ran for the mansion.

I ran so hard that my side hurt, but I didn't slow down. Not until Ashley and I were back in the kitchen, safe and sound— and slimy.

"My heart is beating about five million times a minute," Ashley said as we crossed the kitchen. We stopped to wash up quickly in the big kitchen sink. Then we stepped into the hallway—and froze.

There was music playing somewhere nearby. There hadn't been any music when we sneaked out.

"I think it's coming from that room

across the hall," Ashley whispered.

"That's the library," I told her.

We tiptoed toward the sound. The door to the room was open. I took a quick peek inside. Milo sat by the fireplace. He was reading a book.

"This is perfect," I whispered to Ashley. "Now we can search his room for clues!"

"Do you think we should?" she asked. "Going through someone's stuff isn't very cool."

"But the princess may be in danger," I reminded her. "We have to find out who kidnapped her as fast as we can."

Ashley nodded. We flew up the stairs and down the long hallways to Milo's room.

"You take the dresser. I'll take the closet," Ashley said.

I rushed over to the dresser. I yanked open the top drawer. This search had to be fast. We didn't know how long Milo would be downstairs.

All I found in the top drawer were socks, ties, and underwear. I shut the drawer and opened the next one. There was a whole stack of new shirts. They were all still in plastic wrappers.

I ran my fingers between each pair of shirts in the pile. "Yes!" I cried when I felt between the third and fourth shirt. There was something round in there. Round and hard.

I pulled it out and grinned. It was the proof that we needed—another smoke bomb!

"Put that down, right this second!" a voice cried.

SQUARE ONE

I jumped away from the dresser and turned around. Milo stood in the doorway. His face was bright red. "I said, put that down!" he yelled. "You have no right to be in my room."

"Where is Princess Glorianna?" I cried. "We know you're the one who kidnapped her."

"You set off one of the smoke bombs in her room. You were hoping it would help you sneak the princess away," Ashley

added. "But you weren't expecting her to use the fire extinguisher so quickly."

"That's not true!" Milo exclaimed.

I held the smoke bomb up and shook my head. "This was in *your* drawer. It was hidden between *your* shirts. And it's exactly the kind of smoke bomb that was set off in the princess's room."

Milo stepped into the room and shut the door behind him. "I did set off the smoke bomb," he admitted. "When the princess stepped out for a minute." His voice was low and shaky. "But only to make my film more exciting."

He sat down on the bed. "I knew that Princess Glorianna was an expert in fire safety. It's in her biography," he explained. "So I thought it would be great to get some film of her putting out a fire. Like a hero."

Ashley narrowed her eyes as she stared at him. "You know what would make your movie even *more* exciting?" she asked.

"How about a real, live kidnapping?"

Milo groaned. "You have to believe me. I didn't kidnap the princess. And if she's not back by the time the ball starts, I'm in big trouble!"

"Why?" I asked.

"The queen wants the princess's ball to be the last scene of the movie. She says that's what will make people want to watch it," Milo explained. "She'll fire me if I don't get the ball on film."

Ashley and I looked at each other. I wasn't sure if Milo was telling the truth. I could tell Ashley wasn't sure either.

"I have proof." Milo jumped up. He grabbed his jacket from the back of a chair. Then he pulled a letter out of his pocket.

He pushed it at Ashley. "Here. Read it!"

Ashley unfolded the letter. She read in silence for a moment. "The queen does say that the ball has to be the ending of the movie," she told me. "It also says that the

movie should be happy. It should make people feel good."

"And watching a princess put out a fire *would* make people feel good," Milo cried. "But a movie about Princess Glorianna getting kidnapped would make everyone feel terrible."

"We believe you," I told Milo.

"But setting off a smoke bomb was not smart," Ashley told him. "People panic when they think there is a fire. Somebody could have gotten hurt."

"I'll never do it again. I promise," Milo answered.

"Fine," I said, and started toward the door.

"Where are you going?" Milo asked.

"To find the princess," Ashley told him.

"Hey," Milo called after us. "How would you two like me to make a movie about you? Twin detectives! I can see it now!"

"No, thanks," I said. Who knew what

Milo would do to us to make his movie more exciting!

Ashley and I hurried out into the hall. "We only have one suspect left," Ashley said.

"The duke," I agreed. "But how do we get proof that he's the one who kidnapped the princess?"

"Let's go to his room right now," Ashley answered. "Maybe he's awake. We might get some clues if we talk to him."

We were getting to know our way around the mansion pretty well. It only took us a minute to get to the duke's room. The door was closed.

I pressed my ear against the door. "I think I hear someone crying in there," I said.

"Maybe it's Princess Glorianna," Ashley whispered. "Maybe the duke never even took her out of the mansion!" She pressed her ear against the door.

Whoops! It swung open.

The duke looked up at us from his seat at his desk. His face was streaked with tears. He didn't look dangerous. He just looked sad.

"What's wrong?" Ashley exclaimed.

"Are you sick?" I asked him.

"I've let down the king and queen!" he sobbed. "And I've put Princess Glorianna in danger."

"What do you mean?" Ashley demanded.

"I should never have been made head of security," he said. "I'm no good at it. Glorianna never would have been kidnapped if I'd been more careful."

I noticed a box of tissues on the desk. I hurried over to get one and then handed it to him. He blew his nose loudly.

"What's this?" I asked. I pointed to a photo of Princess Glorianna on the duke's computer screen.

The duke sniffled. "It's my Princess

71

Glorianna Web site," he answered. His eyes filled with tears again. "The princess is so kind. She knew I'd lost almost all my money in a bad business deal. And she…"

I handed him a few more tissues. He blew his nose again.

"She told me I could sell locks of her hair and other memorabilia. Photos. Hair ribbons. Autographs," the duke said. "Lots of places sell fake Princess Glorianna items. But mine would be the only ones that were completely authorized by Princess Glorianna herself."

The duke grabbed another tissue. He wiped his eyes. "She was so good to me. And now…now she's gone. And I can't even figure out who kidnapped her!"

"Don't worry. We're going to get her back," I promised him.

"We're detectives," Ashley added. "And we're on the case."

I patted the duke on the shoulder. Then

Ashley and I hurried out of the room. I shut the door behind us.

"Poor guy," I said.

"Yeah. I think we can take him off our list of suspects," Ashley said. "He can't make money on his Web site if Glorianna is missing!"

I nodded. "You're right. Kidnapping the princess would destroy his business. She's the one who supplies the stuff he sells. Besides, he seems to really care about her."

I sighed. "I'm glad the duke isn't the kidnapper," I said. "But we used to have three great suspects."

"Yeah," Ashley said gloomily. "And now we have zero."

11

JUST LIKE NORMAL

Ashley and I walked back down to our room. I sat down on my bed. "What do we do now?" I asked.

"I don't know," Ashley said. "We don't have any suspects left. And we're out of clues." She shrugged. "I'll read more of Princess Glorianna's biography out loud. Maybe that will give us some ideas."

I leaned back on the pillows. Ashley flipped open the book.

"Here's a direct quote from Princess

Glorianna," Ashley said. "She says, 'I love being a princess. I'm proud to serve my country and my people. But sometimes I wish I could have a normal life. Go to a regular school. Go to the movies. Do the things that a normal kid would do.'"

"She really likes normal stuff," I commented. "Remember how much she loved Serena's orange sneakers?"

"Yeah," Ashley agreed. "The princess's golden slippers are beautiful. But I can see why she'd get tired of wearing them every single day."

"She wasn't wearing them when she was kidnapped," I pointed out. "At least, not both of them." I shook my head. "I still don't get why she was only wearing one slipper. It's weird!"

Ashley sat up. "That's not the only weird thing," she said. "*None* of Glorianna's clothes were missing when Serena checked them. Not even her pajamas! That means the princess wasn't wearing *any* of her own clothes when she was kidnapped."

I shook my head. "That doesn't make sense!"

"Hmmm," Ashley said. "Hmmm. Hmmm." Sometimes she says "hmmm" a lot when she's thinking hard.

"I have an idea!" I sat up and faced Ashley. "I bet the kidnapper wanted to make the princess look as different as possible. Otherwise, someone would spot her."

"Right!" Ashley exclaimed. "She would look a lot different in regular clothes. No fancy dress. No golden slippers."

"Yeah," I agreed. "She'd look like a totally normal girl."

"A totally normal girl," Ashley repeated.

We both gasped.

"Are you thinking what I'm thinking?" I asked.

"I think so. Are you thinking maybe the princess kidnapped *herself*?" Ashley asked.

"Yes!" I cried. "I even know where she got the clothes. She took Serena's orange sneakers because she really loved them."

"And Jen's sweatshirt. And the jeans and the sunglasses and the baseball cap from the other kids," Ashley added.

"Yeah!" I said. "Then she faked that kidnap note, and broke her own window…"

"And threw her slipper out so we'd think the kidnappers took her out that way," Ashley finished. "It all makes sense now!"

I grinned. "We just solved two mysteries at once," I exclaimed. "The Case of the Missing Princess, *and* the Case of the Missing Clothes!"

"The two cases aren't really solved yet," Ashley told me. "Not until we get the princess back. And the clothes!"

"So we have to figure out where Princess Glorianna went after she kidnapped herself," I said.

"She was really interested in the amusement park, remember?" Ashley asked. "She asked us if we'd ever been to one like it."

I jumped to my feet. "The amusement park is right near the mansion." I checked the clock. "It's still open, too. Mom told me it doesn't close until midnight."

"We have to tell the duke," Ashley cried. "Let's go!"

The duke pulled the limo up to the main gates of the Red Balloons Amusement Park. "Are you sure this is the right place?" he asked.

"Princess Glorianna is here. I know it," I said.

"You stay here," Ashley said. "It might be better for me and Mary-Kate to look for the princess on our own."

"You're the experts," he answered.

Ashley and I climbed out of the limo. We stood in front of the gates. I tried to notice each person who left. It was hard. There

were a lot of people in the crowd.

"The amusement park will be closing in five minutes," a voice said over the loud-speaker.

"Where are you, Princess Glorianna?" Ashley whispered.

All the faces started to blur together. I decided to look at feet instead. Orange sneakers would be hard to miss.

"There's a red pair," I muttered. "A white pair. Another white pair. Green pair. Plaid pair. Black pair. Orange pair!"

I grabbed Ashley by the shoulder. "Orange sneakers!" I shouted. We pushed our way through the crowd. I didn't let my eyes leave the orange sneakers.

Finally the sneakers were right in front of me. I looked up. Then I let out a sigh of relief.

"I should have known Olsen and Olsen would find me," Princess Glorianna said.

THE RED CARPET TREATMENT

The next evening, Ashley, Serena, and I gathered in Princess Glorianna's room. She had a surprise for us before the ball.

"I'm giving you all tiaras to wear tonight," Princess Glorianna told us. She smiled at me, Ashley, and Serena.

I looked at all the glittering tiaras laid out on her bed. "Go ahead," the princess urged. "Pick one! We're going to a ball. It's tiara time!"

"Me? In a real tiara?" I asked.

The princess laughed. "Yes, you!" She studied my face a minute. "You should wear this one, Mary-Kate."

Princess Glorianna picked up a thin circle of gold leaves. She placed it carefully on my head. Then she waved Ashley over. "And for you—stars," she said.

Ashley smiled as the princess picked up a circle of silver stars. Glorianna smiled back as she set it on Ashley's head. "It looks perfect with your dress," she said.

Then the princess picked up a tiara covered with diamonds. "I know this one is your favorite," she told Serena.

"Thanks, Glorianna!" Serena squealed.

"Yesterday I realized how fun it can be to borrow clothes," Princess Glorianna said. "Although I guess it wasn't exactly *borrowing*. I didn't ask or anything."

"It's okay," Ashley said. "You gave everything back."

"And you bought everyone souvenirs at

the amusement park," I added.

"I don't think my uncle really liked the stuffed puppy I gave him," Glorianna said. "Or maybe he's still mad at me for what I did," she added with a sigh.

"He was really worried about you," I said. "Everyone was."

Glorianna nodded. "I know—and I'm sorry. Next time I go off on my own, I'll make sure I tell people the truth about it."

Princess Glorianna turned toward the mirror. She gave her hair a quick pat. "Time to go downstairs."

"We need to go first," Serena explained to Ashley and me. "Glorianna has to come down the stairs by herself. It gives everyone a chance to look at her."

Ashley, Serena, and I headed out the door. The skirts of our long gowns *swoosh*ed as we walked.

We paused when we reached the top of the long staircase that led to the ballroom.

Ashley gave a happy sigh. "It's so awesome," she exclaimed.

"Amazing!" I agreed. A huge chandelier hung over the center of the dance floor. It sparkled as brightly as the diamonds on Serena's tiara.

"Look at the fountain!" Ashley cried. "I can see goldfish in it."

"And those are real trees," I said, pointing to a corner of the ballroom. "I love the twinkly lights on the branches."

"Let's go down," Serena said.

"I feel like Cinderella," Ashley whispered as we followed Serena down the stairs.

"That's exactly what I was thinking," I whispered back.

The orchestra began to play as we reached the main floor. Then Princess Glorianna came slowly down the stairs. The crowd *ooohed*. Flashbulbs went off. Milo didn't stop filming for a second. I pointed him out to Ashley.

"His movie is going to have a happy ending after all," Ashley said with a grin.

The princess walked over to us. "How do you like your first ball?" she asked me and Ashley.

"This is so incredible," Ashley replied. "Would you really give all this up to be a normal kid?"

"No. I had a wonderful day as a normal girl," Princess Glorianna answered. "But I wouldn't trade my life for anyone else's. I love making people's lives better."

"Like with your fire safety TV commercials," I said.

"Yes," the princess answered. She reached out and touched Serena on the arm. "I wish you could be a princess, too. I know you love all of—"

"Don't worry about it," Serena interrupted. "I've figured out what I *really* want to be. A detective, like Mary-Kate and Ashley!"

Ashley and I laughed.

Serena did a little bounce on her toes. "I'm going to get some rubber gloves," she added. "The kind detectives on TV wear. Mittens are too hot."

"Good idea," Ashley said.

"I'd better go," Princess Glorianna told us. "I need to say hello to all the guests."

I watched her walk away. Her golden slippers shone with each step. And each person she passed smiled a little more brightly.

The princess crossed the room to the stage. She climbed the steps. Then she walked over to the orchestra conductor and whispered in his ear.

The conductor stepped up to the microphone. "Ladies and gentlemen," he said. "Princess Glorianna of Pomeroy would like to say something to you all."

He pulled the microphone off its stand. Then he handed it to the princess.

"Good evening, everyone. And welcome," Princess Glorianna said. "I hope you have a wonderful time tonight. I'd just like to make a quick announcement before we begin our evening."

The ballroom was absolutely silent. Every eye was on the princess.

"My uncle and I made a very important decision this afternoon. We've chosen a special royal security team," she said. "They will be responsible for my safety whenever I travel in America. Their names are Mary-Kate and Ashley Olsen."

I let out a squeak of surprise.

Princess Gloriana smiled at us. "If that's okay with you two, I mean."

Ashley and I looked at each other. Then we turned back to the princess.

"It's more than okay!" we said together.

Princess Glorianna gave the conductor a nod. "Let the ball begin!" she cried.

Hi from both of us,

Break out the dancing shoes! Ashley and I got invited to a 1920s party at the house of a famous mystery writer, Fiona O'Leary. We couldn't wait to wear cool '20s costumes for the big dance contest. We were totally psyched for an evening of flapping and fun.

But then Fiona's adored cat, Flapper, disappeared. And everyone thought our dog Clue dunnit! Ashley and I were sure Clue was innocent—but we had to prove it. And fast—or Olsen and Olsen might end up Clue-less!

Want to find out more? Check out the next page for a sneak peek at The New Adventures of Mary-Kate & Ashley: *The Case of the Flapper 'Napper*.

See you next time!

Mary-Kate Olsen   *Ashley Olsen*

The Case Of The
FLAPPER 'NAPPER

The library doors swung open, just as Fiona O'Leary was about to start reading from one of her mystery books. Shirley, the maid, stood in the doorway. She looked pale and very, very scared.

"Madam!" Shirley cried. "It's Flapper. She's…she's…missing!"

"My kitty!" Fiona put her hand to her heart and made little gasping noises. "It can't be. It just can't be!"

"Don't worry, Mrs. O'Leary," Ashley said quickly. "Mary-Kate and I will help you find Flapper."

"Let's look around Flapper's room first," I said. "Maybe we can find some clues in there."

The two of us dashed out of the library and up the stairs. "You don't think anyone got rid of Flapper, do you?" Ashley asked in a low voice as we hurried down the hallway.

I shrugged. "I don't know," I whispered. "Is there anyone who *likes* Fiona's precious pet?"

We rushed into Flapper's room. Fiona was right behind us.

Ashley and I couldn't believe our eyes! There was a blue satin kitty bed, a white furry scratching post, and a big white tub. The tub was surrounded by bottles of Pretty Kitty Bubble Bath.

And in the middle of everything was our very own Clue. She was lying on Flapper's bed. She looked very comfortable.

Fiona narrowed her eyes. "I think we've found the culprit!" she announced. "It's... *that dog!*"

PSSST —The Secret's Out!

The Trenchcoat Twins™ Are Solving Brand-New Mysteries!

Watch Mary-Kate & Ashley's Adventures on Fox Family Channel on Saturday mornings!

The New Adventures of MARY-KATE & ASHLEY

The Case Of The SUMMER CAMP CAPER
The Case Of The Surfing Secret
The Case Of The GREEN GHOST
The Case Of The Big Scary Halloween Mystery
The Case Of The SLAM DUNK MYSTERY
Rock Star
The Case Of The CHEERLEADING CAMP
The Case Of The Flying PHANTOM
Creepy Castle
The Case Of The GOLDEN Slipper
FLAPPER NAPPER

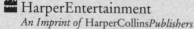

READ THEM ALL!

At bookstores everywhere, or call 1-800-331-3761 to order.

HarperEntertainment
An Imprint of HarperCollins*Publishers*
www.harpercollins.com

outta-site!
marykateandashley.com
Register Now

Books created and produced by Parachute Publishing, L.L.C.,
in cooperation with Dualstar Publications, a division of Dualstar Entertainment Group, Inc.
The New Adventures of Mary-Kate & Ashley TM & © 2000 Dualstar Entertainment Group, Inc.

PARACHUTE PRESS

DUALSTAR PUBLICATIONS

HANG OUT WITH

MARY-KATE & ASHLEY

in their cool
book series

BASED ON THE TV SERIES!

COLLECT THEM ALL!

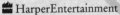

outta-site!
marykateandashley.com
Register Now

At bookstores everywhere,
or call 1-800-331-3761 to order.

Books created and produced by Parachute Publishing, L.L.C., in cooperation
with Dualstar Publications, a division of Dualstar Entertainment Group, Inc.
TWO OF A KIND TM & © 2000 Warner Bros.

HarperEntertainment
An Imprint of HarperCollinsPublishers
www.harpercollins.com

PARACHUTE PRESS

DUALSTAR PUBLICATIONS

Can Mary-Kate and Ashley Keep a Secret?
Find out in their NEW movie

Mary-Kate Olsen   **Ashley Olsen**

Our Lips Are Sealed

Filmed in Sydney, Australia

DUALSTAR
VIDEO

TM & © 2000 Dualstar Entertainment Group, Inc. Distributed by Warner Home Video.

ADVERTISEMENT

Double the fashion! Double the fun!

with Mary-Kate & Ashley Fashion Dolls

Mary-Kate and ASHLEY

Ride with Mary-Kate

Dance with Ashley

Join their slumber party

outta-site!
marykateandashley.com
Register Now

In Stores Now!

DUALSTAR
CONSUMER PRODUCTS

MATTEL

Each doll sold separately and comes with two extra fashions. Subject to availability.
TM & ©1999 Dualstar Entertainment Group, Inc. All Rights Reserved. ©1999 Mattel, Inc. All Rights Reserved.

mary-kateandashley
Magical Mystery Mall™

October

2000

Available Now

PlayStation

DUALSTAR INTERACTIVE

Outta-site!
marykateandashley.com
Register Now

GAME BOY COLOR

RATING PENDING
RP
CONTENT RATED BY
ESRB

CLUB ACCLAIM

© & TM 2000 Dualstar Entertainment Group, Inc., Acclaim® and Club Acclaim™ & © 2000 Acclaim Entertainment, Inc. All Rights Reserved. Marketed by Acclaim, Distributed by Acclaim Distribution Inc. One Acclaim Plaza, Glen Cove, NY 11542-2777. PlayStation and the PlayStation logos are registered trademarks of Sony Computer Entertainment Inc. Game Boy and Game Boy Color are trademarks of Nintendo of America Inc. © 1989, 1998 Nintendo of America Inc. Licensed by Nintendo.

Listen To Us!

Greates

Ballet Party™

t Hits

Birthday Party™

Sleepover Party™

Brother For Sale™

Mary-Kate & Ashley's CDs and Cassettes Available Now Wherever Music is Sold

I Am The Cute One™

LIGHTYEAR
Lightyear Entertainment

DUALSTAR RECORDS

Distributed in the U.S. by
wea

TMs & ©℗2000 Dualstar Records.

outta site!
marykateandashley.com™
Register Now

TM & © 2000 Dualstar Entertainment Group Inc.

Check out
the Reading Room on
marykateandashley.com
for an exclusive
online chapter preview
of our upcoming book!

DUALSTAR
ONLINE

TM & © 2000 Dualstar Entertainment Group, Inc. All Rights Reserved.